Adapted by Alice Alfonsi

Based on the series created by Michael Poryes and Susan Sherman

Part One is based on the episode, "A Goat's Tale," Written by Ed Evans

Part Two is based on the episode, "Boyz 'N Commotion," Written by Theresa Akana & Stacee Comage

New York

Printed in the United States of America

First Edition
1 3 5 7 9 10 8 6 4 2

Library of Congress Control Number on file.

ISBN 13: 978-0-7868-3839-4
ISBN 10: 0-7868-3839-6

For more Disney Press fun, visit www.disneybooks.com
Visit DisneyChannel.com

Part One

Chapter One

Wow! These call-in contests are intense! Chelsea Daniels thought. She was huddled with some girls in the Bayside cafeteria. All of them were listening intently to a small radio.

"Okay," the DJ finally announced, "we know you're pumped about tonight's Boyz 'N Motion, 'Motion at Midnight' concert. And we're giving away all-access wristbands to our *tenth* caller!"

All-access wristbands! Chelsea thought. Awesome!

Every girl within earshot whipped out her cell phone. Chelsea joined the speed-dialing posse. But she'd barely pressed the SEND button before the DJ said, "No more calls. We have a winner!"

Chelsea stomped her foot. "Oh, man! C'mon! What do you have to be, like, *psychic* to win these contests?"

Truer words were never spoken because Bayside's very own teen psychic *had* won.

"Caller number ten in the hizz-ouse!" Raven Baxter shouted. Rushing into the cafeteria, she waved her cell phone like a victory flag.

With a chorus of groans, the speed-dialing girls shut off their cells and put them away.

"Boyz 'N Motion tickets are going to be in my hands, people," Raven said, tossing back her long, brown ponytail. "I am going to the concert!"

"Aw, this is so unfair," Chelsea said. "I wanted to go."

Still grinning, Raven walked over to her best friend. "Chels, I won *two* tickets."

"Sure, Rae, rub it in."

Raven sighed. Chelsea was the sweetest,

most loyal friend. Unfortunately, in the brain department, the girl's shelves weren't always what you'd call *fully stocked.*

"Okay, let's start this over again," said Raven, smoothing the lapels of her long suede jacket. "Hey, Chels, you want to go to the concert *with me*?" She made sure to emphasize the "with me" part.

Chelsea's eyes widened with happy surprise. "Wow, Rae! It's kind of out of *nowhere,* but sure, yeah!"

"Out of nowhere?" Raven repeated to herself. Where's this girl been for the last ten minutes? Outer space?

"This will be great!" said Chelsea.

"Yes, it will," said Raven. She was totally psyched now and began bustin' the band's trademark dance moves. Chelsea joined in.

"Boyz!" they cried with an on-beat foot stomp. "We are the Boyz 'N Motion." *Clap!*

"We give you our devotion. Boyz!" *Stomp!* "We are the Boyz 'N Motion." *Clap!* "We give you our—"

"Pssst," a voice interrupted. "Bring your motion over here."

Raven and Chelsea stopped their stomping and clapping. Eddie Thomas was tiptoeing toward them.

"C'mere," he whispered, waving them over.

Raven exchanged a confused glance with Chelsea. The last time Eddie had acted this weird in the lunch room he'd accidentally eaten half the waxed fruit off the Art Club's "Bountiful Seasons" display.

"You okay, Eddie?" Raven asked, walking up to him.

"Yeah . . ." Eddie glanced around worriedly, as if he didn't want anyone to overhear. "I did the coolest thing," he whispered.

"Aw, Eddie," said Chelsea, grinning. "Your homework? A-plus!" She gave him a thumbs-up.

Eddie rolled his eyes. "It's not my homework. Just follow me." He led the girls out of the cafeteria and down an empty hall to a school storage room.

"Okay," he told them, "you know how every year, before the big game against Jefferson, they steal our mascot, Barry Barracuda, right?"

Raven nodded.

Chelsea stared blankly. "No," she said.

Eddie's fists clenched. "Chelsea, *why* must you make everything so *difficult?*"

"Eddie," Raven interrupted, "what did you do?"

Eddie unclenched a fist and grabbed hold of the storage room's doorknob. "Okay, this year," he whispered, "I stole *their* mascot."

Flinging open the door, he announced,

"Ladies, meet Gomez, the Jefferson mascot!"

Raven gaped at the sight in front of her. The little animal stood no more than two feet high. It had a black furry hide and cute floppy ears. A bright red Jefferson Patriots varsity sweater covered its torso and a tricornered hat sat on its little head.

Raven turned back to face Eddie. "You stole a goat?"

"Yeah," he said, "but it's only until after the game, okay? I mean, without their mascot, they'll be totally psyched out. We'll finally *beat* 'em, Rae."

Raven rolled her eyes. "We couldn't beat 'em if we stole the whole team!"

Bayside had one of worst football teams in the county, and Jefferson had one of the best. Stealing their mascot wasn't going to help Bayside win a game. And Raven didn't have to be psychic to know that!

"Baaaa, baaaa," bleated Gomez.

"You know what?" Chelsea said. "This *stinks*."

"Yeah," Raven agreed, sniffing the air. "Gomez is kind of ripe."

"No, Rae," said Chelsea. She crouched down and began to pet the little goat. "What stinks is making an innocent animal parade around in this ridiculous outfit."

"You know, Chelsea's right," said Raven, checking out the red sweater and tricornered hat. "That hat is *so* seventeen seventy-six! Ha-ha! Seventeen seventy-six!"

Raven laughed. Eddie laughed, too. But Chelsea didn't even crack a smile. In fact, she started frowning.

"Get it?" Raven nudged Chelsea. "Seventeen seventy-six!" She marched like a minuteman and gave a salute to help Chelsea with the joke. Then she laughed some more. But Chelsea's frown only deepened.

"Okay, okay. Rae, you know what?" she said, standing up to face her. "You can laugh all you want, but animals are creatures, okay? With feelings, you know? . . ." She glanced down at Gomez. ". . . Who also happen to be really hungry."

Eddie folded his arms. "And how do *you* know?"

"Uh, Eddie?" Raven interrupted.

"What?" he snapped. After all the trouble he'd gone to, Eddie thought the girls would be congratulating him, not dissing him!

Raven pointed to his trousers. "You're kind of lackin' in the backin'."

"Lackin' in the backin'?" Eddie repeated. What's that supposed to mean? he wondered. Then he turned around and found out.

"Oh, Gomez!" he cried.

Gomez the goat had been snacking on

whatever was in Eddie's back pocket, along with the pocket itself. Now Eddie was left with a big hole in the seat of his pants.

Dang, thought Raven. Between that out-of-date hat and Eddie's peekaboo trousers, that goat's a four-legged fashion disaster!

Later that day, Bayside held a pep rally in the gym. Everyone was so pumped, they kept on cheering as they headed back into the hallway.

"Bayside is bad. Go, Bayside!" cried the cheerleaders. "Bayside is bad. Go, Bayside. Bayside is bad. Go, Bayside!"

As the cheerleaders kicked and the crowd clapped, Eddie leaped onto the main staircase. This was it! His big moment. He called for everyone's attention.

The students, cheerleaders, and members of the football team were now staring at him. Big D, the team captain, folded his massive arms.

"All right, okay, all right!" Eddie cried. "Now I am sick and tired of Jefferson stealing our mascot every year before the big game."

Kids in the crowd nodded and murmured in agreement.

"This year it's not going to happen," Eddie declared.

As the crowd cheered, the student wearing the Barry Barracuda costume danced around and pumped his fist in the air.

"Well, we've been keeping a very watchful eye on Barry Barracuda!" Eddie proclaimed.

As the kids whooped and clapped, two big Jefferson football players snuck into the hallway. They took hold of Barry and pulled him right out the school's back door!

The cheering Bayside students failed to notice they'd just lost their mascot—*again*. So did Eddie. He just kept going on with his speech.

"Well, Jefferson should have been watching their own mascot, Gomez the goat!" he cried.

Big D unfolded his massive arms and stared down at Eddie. "Thomas, did you steal the goat?"

Eddie grinned with pride. "Well, uh, Big D, let's just say that this school is about to get some very long-overdue respect. Fellow Barracudas, I give you . . ."

Eddie waved to Raven. He'd already asked her to stand by the storage room door and open it on cue. Now he called out, "Rae!"

She opened the door. But when she looked inside the storeroom, all she saw were school supplies. "Your stinkin' goat ain't in there," she called back to Eddie.

"What?!" Eddie cried. He rushed over. "It can't be!"

Raven went back inside the storeroom and came out again. "But here," she said, handing him an old mop. "This is good enough, right?"

It seemed like a fair exchange to her. After all, the mop certainly smelled as nasty as that goat!

But the pep-rally posse didn't agree. They groaned in disappointment. And nobody was more disappointed than Big D and his football crew. The giant players glared at Eddie and his mop.

"The game's tonight, Thomas." Big D poked Eddie's shoulder. "You had us all pumped. Now we're *bummed*. And we don't win when we're bummed."

"Man," said Raven, narrowing her eyes at the bully. "Y'all must have been bummed *every* game, 'cause y'all *never*—"

"Rae, Rae, Rae, Rae," Eddie interrupted. "I got this, okay?" He faced the football team's captain. "Don't worry, Big D, okay? That goat's going to be at the game, dog, sorry. . . ."

"Well, it better be," Big D warned, "'cause if you don't find it, I'm going to find *you*." He poked Eddie's shoulder again, this time even harder. Then he turned to his teammates. "Let's go!"

Raven shook her head as Big D and his *lame*-dog, touchdown-challenged teammates walked away. "Why are you so mean?" she asked them. "We're just trying to help you out!"

Big D ignored her. So did the other players. They all followed Big D down the hall. The cheerleaders and pep-club posse trailed behind them.

"Okay, all right," Eddie said, trying to stay upbeat. "Hey, look at all the pretty ladies, following Big D. Okay, Big D!" he called after him with a nervous grin. But as soon as they were gone, Eddie panicked. He turned to Raven.

"Rae, what are we going to do?"

"Oooh," Raven stepped back. Normally, she'd have Eddie's back. But this goat-snatching business was nasty. And the Boyz 'N Motion concert was *tonight!*

"I don't know about 'we,'" she told him, "but *me's* going to the concert." And with a final peace-out sign for her unhappy homeboy, Raven was gone.

Chapter Two

"Oh, Dad!" Cory Baxter cried after school that afternoon. "I'm right on your tail!"

Chase Thru Space! was Cory's favorite new computer game. Using planets and asteroids, a player could shield his own spaceship while shooting at his opponent's. The highest score won—and Cory *always* got the highest score.

"Yes!" he shouted, his chubby little fingers wildly working the plastic joystick. "Your ship is vaporized!"

Sitting next to his son on the living room sofa, Mr. Baxter shook his head. "It's not over yet," he said. "I've still got two ships left!"

Cory furiously worked his joystick.

"Okay, one ship," his dad corrected and

brought out his last resort. Two seconds later, he said, "Okay, *no* ships. Game's over."

Cory cracked his knuckles. I *rule*, he thought. My undefeated title remains intact!

"I think I need some real competition," he announced. "I'm going to play on the Internet." As his teacher said, the World Wide Web was a communications miracle. Cory couldn't have agreed more. "Now I can crush kids from all over the world!"

"Well, keep in mind, the world's a big place," Mr. Baxter warned. "You *might* lose."

Me? Lose? Cory thought. He busted out laughing. "Ha-ha. Good one, Dad!"

Cory hit the button for his Internet connection. "Okay, bring it on," he murmured to the digital world. "Let's see who's out there."

He tapped the keys on his laptop, looking for a willing victim. "Oh, I've got someone . . . in Hong Kong!" He read the screen to see his opponent's name. "Jing Yee."

Halfway around the world, a little girl about Cory's age was sitting at her bedroom desk, studying her own laptop screen.

"Cory," Jing Yee read. Then she smiled, spit on each small palm and rubbed them together. "Finally, some competition," she murmured in Cantonese.

Back in San Francisco, Cory was smiling, too. "Let the game begin!" he cried.

Raven crossed her backyard and pushed open the kitchen door. Man, was she glad to be home. Eddie was totally buggin' over that silly goat, and she wanted to chill before the concert. But peace and quiet wasn't exactly what she got when she walked into her house.

"Rae!" her mom cried, rushing up to her with wild eyes. "A messenger brought this for you this afternoon!"

Mrs. Baxter held out a small blue envelope. Raven noticed the radio station's call letters engraved in the corner. She excitedly ripped open the seal.

"It's the Boyz 'N Motion wristbands!" she shouted.

Mrs. Baxter started jumping up and down. "I can't believe you were the tenth caller!"

Raven stepped back in confusion. "Mom, you were listening?"

Mrs. Baxter nodded. "I've been trying to get in all afternoon. That's why there's no dinner."

Raven was really touched. How many mothers would spend hours trying to win concert tickets for her teenage daughter?

"Mommy, can you believe it?" Raven took her mom's hands, and they both began dancing around the kitchen. "Boyz 'N Motion, 'Motion at Midnight'!"

"I know!" Mrs. Baxter cried, her braids flying in every direction. "It's so exciting. You know, I should take a nap before the limo comes."

"Why?" Raven asked.

Her mother stopped dancing. "So I won't be tired when the Boyz start their motions," Mrs. Baxter replied. Then she started getting jiggy again.

"Uh-oh," said Raven. "Mama, come here."

But Mrs. Baxter just kept bustin' moves around the kitchen—and from what Raven could see, most of those moves weren't what you'd call *fresh*.

When her mom finally calmed down, Raven put a hand on her shoulder. "You know I love you," she said. "And I want to thank you for bringing me into this world. *Thank you*. But . . . how can I say this nicely? You *ain't* going."

Her mom looked crushed, and Raven suddenly felt terrible. "I'm sorry. I'm sorry," she quickly added. "But I already promised Chelsea."

"Oh." Her mom nodded. She seemed to understand. "Oh, well," she said with a shrug, "I'm still taking a nap. There's been a little too much *motion* for Mama."

Raven laughed, and so did her mother. Then the two hugged.

"You girls have fun," said Mrs. Baxter.

Knock! Knock!

Raven turned to find Chelsea peeking in through the back-door window. "Hey, Rae," she said as Raven opened the door. "Can I see you outside for a minute?"

"Outside?" Raven asked. "Why?"

"Well, because . . ." said Chelsea a little nervously. "I don't think he's really allowed in the house."

Raven's eyes narrowed suspiciously. "He *who*?"

Chelsea led Raven into the Baxters' backyard. There, eating his way through Mrs. Baxter's petunias, was Eddie's missing goat.

"You stole the goat?!" Raven cried.

"I didn't steal him Rae, okay?" Chelsea said defensively. "I liberated him."

"Well, you need to *unliberate* him," Raven warned.

"Okay, listen, Rae, I can't." Chelsea bent down to stroke the goat's soft, black coat. "I can't send him back to a life of shame and humiliation, you know, and really cheesy halftime shows!"

Raven could see Gomez was no longer wearing his mascot uniform. Obviously Chelsea had tossed the red Jefferson sweater and tricornered hat. She'd also put a leash on him, as if he were some kind of puppy!

Raven shook her head. This is totally messed up, she thought. "Chels, you can*not* keep him here."

"Rae, it's cool," Chelsea insisted, "'cause I've got it all worked out. All we have to do is take him to a farm tonight."

"We?" Raven threw up her hands. All this goat-snatching was ruining her social life. "Why is 'me' always included in 'we'? No, listen. The only thing 'we' are going to do is go to the *concert.*"

Just then, Eddie walked into Raven's backyard. "Chelsea!" He shook his head. "I knew I'd find that goat with you."

Chelsea quickly stepped in front of the little animal. "What goat?"

"Nice try, Chels," Eddie said. Then he lunged at her. "Give up the goat!"

"No, no, no, never!" Chelsea cried. She wrapped her arms around him and nodded toward Raven. "We are taking him to a farm, okay?"

Raven groaned. "Chelsea, okay, *again*—the *we*."

"Look, Chels," said Eddie, "don't you get it? If Gomez isn't at that game, there's going to be some very large, very angry people looking for me."

Chelsea stood her ground. "Eddie, listen, animals are living creatures, okay? They deserve respect and dignity."

"Absolutely," he said. "Now, what did you do with his funny-looking hat?" Eddie pretended to be looking around for the tri-cornered patriot hat. Then he suddenly moved to grab the goat's leash. "Okay, Gomez! Let's go!"

"No, no, no," Chelsea said, chasing after Eddie. She grabbed back the leash, and Eddie lunged for it again.

"Hey, stop it! Stop it!" Chelsea cried, lashing Eddie with the strip of leather.

"I *know* you aren't trying to beat me!" Eddie cried.

"Okay, people, people, people!" Raven shouted. "Hey! This is *ridiculous*!" Stepping between her peeps, she halted the tug-of-Gomez war. "It is *just* a *goat*, okay? We need to remember what is important right now . . . Boyz 'N Motion. 'Motion at Midnight.' That is what's important. Now settle this so Chelsea and I can put on our wristbands and . . ."

Raven's voice trailed off as she felt her back pocket. "Where are my wristbands?" she murmured. "Okay, they were in my pocket . . . but where's my *pocket*?"

Raven suddenly realized her pocket had been chewed right off her pants. In total shock, she stared at Gomez. The dang goat struck again! She could see the last few pieces of the radio station's blue envelope in his chomping mouth!

Raven squeezed her eyes shut. "Gomez, Gomez, Gomez! Why?!"

As Raven began to sob in despair, Eddie's cell phone rang. He answered it, and after a few seconds of listening, he quickly said, "Okay, Big D, okay, don't worry. That goat's *going* to be at the game. . . . Or you're going to do *what* to me . . . ?"

Eddie gave a tense laugh. "Come on, dog, now you know that's physically impossible!" A second later he was grimacing. "Oh, you can *make* it work? Well, okay, man. All right, I'll see you at the game. Okay."

Eddie hung up and moaned. "Oh, man . . ." He angrily clenched his fists. "Chelsea, I hope you're happy!"

"Well . . ." Chelsea thought it over. "I'm generally a happy person, I guess." She smiled serenely. "I think it really comes from within."

Eddie bit his tongue to keep from screaming.

"Baaaaaaaaa," bleated Gomez.

In the kitchen, Raven's mom heard the strange sound. She opened the back door and strode into the yard. "What are you kids—" Mrs. Baxter began, then stopped and stared at the little four-legged animal. "That's a *goat*."

"No, Mama," said Raven. "It isn't a goat. It's 'Jaws' in a fur coat!"

Chelsea gasped and put her hands over Gomez's floppy ears. "Hey, Rae, please," she said. "Not in front of the G-O-A-T."

Raven rolled her eyes. "*Hey*, why did he have to E-A-T my wristbands?"

Now Raven's mother gasped. "He A-T-E your wristbands?"

"Yes, Mom," said Raven dejectedly, "and now we can't go to the concert."

"Well, don't give up yet," said Raven's mom. "Goats eat lots of things that are not digestible. And what goes in, must come *out*."

"Oh!" Raven brightened with hope. "You think he'll cough 'em up?"

Mrs. Baxter shook her head. "I was thinking more from the *other* end."

"*Eww*," Raven grimaced at Gomez's furry little tail. "Ya nasty!"

Chapter Three

Two hours later, Cory was still sitting on the living room couch, playing Chase Thru Space! His Hong Kong opponent was hanging tough, and that surprised him. But he'd never once lost his favorite video game, and he was determined to totally crush the competition!

"Gotcha! Gotcha!" he exclaimed, zapping Jing Yee's ship again and again. Then his eyes widened in shock. Where did that ship come from? She must have been hiding it behind an asteroid!

Zap!

"She got *me*?" Cory said in disbelief.

In her Hong Kong bedroom, Jing Yee was

whooping with excitement. "Got him!" she cried in Cantonese.

Meanwhile, the Baxters' backyard had turned into Camp Gomez. Raven had set up a goat-watching station with Chelsea and Eddie. A battery-powered lantern sat on a small wooden table. Sleeping bags and blankets covered the grass.

As Gomez nibbled grass near Chelsea, she petted his soft coat.

Raven checked her watch. She'd waited patiently for two hours. But enough was enough! Picking up the goat's little tail, she addressed his back end. "Come on, you stupid goat. Do you know how many people are waiting for you?"

Eddie sighed in frustration. "Look, man, there's no sense in us just sitting here waiting for something to happen." He rose to his feet.

"Now y'all go ahead inside and get some rest. I'll be a gentleman and take the first watch. Right, Gomez?"

Chelsea eyed him with suspicion. "Ah, no," she told Eddie, getting up herself. "Actually, how 'bout I stay here and watch Gomez, y'know, while *you* guys go someplace really far where you *can't see us.*"

Raven shook her head and stood up, too. "That is a shame. Both of you. I know what you're going to do. I know. As soon as I turn my head, one of y'all is going to snatch that goat!"

"Whoa, Rae!" Chelsea pretended to be deeply wounded. "Are you calling us goat snatchers here?"

"Yeah," said Eddie, looking offended, too.

Raven put her hands on her hips. "You both snatched the goat once already!" she reminded them.

Chelsea and Eddie exchanged guilty glances. "Oh, right. That's true," they murmured.

"Well, if that's the case," said Eddie, sitting down again. "I am not taking my eyes off this goat."

"Well, neither am I," said Chelsea, planting herself right beside him.

Raven stubbornly folded her arms and sat down, too. "Neither am I."

Then the three best friends went back to keeping their eyes on the goat . . . and each other.

As the evening wore on, Cory continued to chase Jing Yee's ships through cyberspace. He was starting to feel fried and hyper, but he refused to give up!

"I'm *not* going to lose to Jing Yee," he murmured, working his joystick. "No way!"

Just then, Mrs. Baxter walked into the living

room. "Cory," she said with alarm, "you have been playing that game for *hours*."

"Mom, please," Cory said, staring intensely at his laptop screen. "One more ship and it's all over."

"Okay," said Mrs. Baxter, returning to the kitchen. "Then wrap it up."

Cory never would have guessed that halfway around the world, Jing Yee was having the very same conversation with her own mother!

"Okay," Jing Yee's mother said, walking into her bedroom. "Finish your game!"

Jing Yee groaned as she worked her joystick. "But, Mom, I have to save my last ship!"

"Okay, then wrap it up," her mother insisted in Cantonese.

For the next few minutes, both kids played their hearts out. Finally, Cory cornered Jing Yee's last ship between an ice asteroid and a blue moon.

"I got you now!" he cried, grinning with glee. "So long, sucker."

Cory sent his ship in for the final kill. And that's when it happened. His lasers stopped firing! "My joystick!" he yelled. "It's not working! I'm a sitting duck!"

"He's a sitting duck," Jing Yee realized. From the other side of the globe, she blasted away at Cory's ship.

Zap! Zap! Pow!

"Game over!" Jing Yee cried.

She'd done it! She'd blown away every last one of Cory's ships.

"Yes! I am victorious." She leaped up and celebrated with her mother, Hong Kong style.

"Who's the boss? Who's the boss? Who's the boss?" the two chanted in Cantonese, as they busted moves around the bedroom.

"Man, it's not right," Cory grumbled.

He held up his computer's joystick, wondering why it had stopped working. That's when he noticed the device's wire. It was frayed and ragged, as if it had been chewed through!

"Baaaaaaaaa!"

Cory looked down at the bleating sound. A furry face stared back up at him. It was still chewing part of his joystick's wire.

"Man," Cory mumbled, "the goat did it."

A split second later, Cory realized what he'd just said. *Oh, snap*, he thought. I did *not* just say—

"The *goat*!" he yelled.

Cory leaped off the couch and ran into the kitchen, where his mom and dad were fixing sandwiches.

"Mom!" he cried. "I just *lost* my game because of a stupid—"

"Cory," his mother sternly interrupted, "it's only a game."

"Yeah," said Cory, "but—"

"Son!" His dad was walking to the kitchen table with a turkey on rye. "You've been bragging and boasting when you're *winning*—"

"But, Dad, there's a—"

Cory's dad didn't want to hear excuses—what he really wanted to do was eat his sandwich. "Listen to me," he said, eyeing the turkey, bacon, lettuce, and mayo. "You need to be a *good sport* and *accept* the fact that somebody just might be better than you."

Cory threw up his hands. He knew when to give up. "Okay! But I still could have taken her if that goat hadn't eaten my joystick."

Mrs. Baxter frowned at her son. She was determined to get through to him. "Cory," she snapped, "you can't blame the goat for—"

"Baaaaaaaaa!"

Cory's mom froze. *Oh, no*, she thought. I did *not* just hear—

"The goat?" said Mr. Baxter.

"In the house?" cried Mrs. Baxter.

"I told y'all," Cory said, pointing to the next room.

His mom and dad rushed out of the kitchen and into the living room. Both stopped in their tracks. The goat had gone on a rampage. Couch pillows had been ripped open. Stuffing was scattered all over the floor. Lamps and tables were overturned. The whole place was wrecked!

Cory was surprised at how quiet his mom and dad had become. Both just stood there, staring, in complete silence.

Wow, he thought, I guess they're not that freaked out after all.

Five seconds later, the shock wore off, and Mrs. Baxter screamed louder than a horror-struck screech owl.

Chapter Four

"**A**aaaaaaaaah! My living room!"

"What was that?" Raven asked, snapping awake on her backyard blanket. She, Eddie, and Chelsea had vowed to keep their eyes on Gomez. But at some point during the evening, every last eyelid had drifted shut.

"Where's Gomez?" Raven asked.

She frantically glanced around the grassy yard, but it was too late. The goat was gone.

"My wristbands!" she cried, leaping off her blanket and running toward the house.

"My mascot!" Eddie yelled, following Raven.

"My baby!" Chelsea bellowed, tailing Eddie.

The three sleepy goat-sitters rushed through

the Baxters' back door and across the kitchen. At the sight of the ruined living room, they came to a dead stop.

"Oh, wow," said Chelsea.

"Oh, man," said Eddie.

"Oh, snap," said Raven.

Cory stepped up to his sister. "Your goat is *so* busted."

"Un-uh. That is not *my* goat." Raven insisted. "That is Eddie's mascot."

Eddie's eyes widened. "Well, it's Chelsea's baby!"

"Y'know what?" said Chelsea. "If Gomez was just on a *farm* where he belongs, he wouldn't have eaten your entire living room!"

"Hey," Mr. Baxter interrupted, "if we don't find him, he's going to eat everything else."

Mrs. Baxter put her hands on her hips. "Goat's not eating *my* house."

Just then, Mr. Baxter spotted Gomez,

hiding behind the sofa. But before he could grab for him, the animal ran into the alcove.

"Ah!" cried Mr. Baxter. "There he goes!"

Everyone rushed toward the alcove, and Gomez trotted into the kitchen. Then everyone raced into the kitchen, and Gomez ran back into the living room!

Mr. Baxter lunged for the little goat. Gomez bolted for the piano, and Raven's dad fell over an ottoman!

Eddie dove to catch his prized mascot, but Gomez was too quick for him. He raced away, heading back toward the open kitchen door.

"Oh, no, you don't!" Cory cried. He leaped to close the door. It worked! Gomez was trapped. But when Raven and Chelsea closed in to grab him, he ran right through Raven's legs!

"Hey!" cried Chelsea, as Raven fell on top of her.

Gomez never looked back. He ran right up the stairs—and Mrs. Baxter started buggin'. All she could see were chewed-up sheets and ruined bed pillows.

"Somebody get that goat!" she cried.

Everybody ran up the stairs. A few minutes later, Cory was running down again, with the goat right behind him!

"Gangway!" Cory cried.

Gomez had eaten so much already, Cory was afraid *he* was next!

Cory ran into the kitchen and leaped onto the counter. Gomez ran out the back door. Now he was right back where he started, in the Baxter's enclosed yard.

Raven's mother followed the little goat into the yard. Raven, Eddie, Chelsea, and Cory ran up behind her. Together, they all cornered Gomez.

Huffing and puffing, Raven's father brought

up the rear. "Okay," he rasped. "We got you now!"

Mr. Baxter was right. The little goat couldn't get out of the fenced-in yard. Chelsea approached the little animal and gently took hold of his collar.

An exhausted Mrs. Baxter shook her finger at Raven, Eddie, and Chelsea. "I thought you kids were watching him!" she said between gasps of fresh night air.

Raven threw up her hands. "Man," she said, "do you know how boring it is to just sit and wait for the goat to do his business?"

"Okay, that's it," said Mr. Baxter. "I want this animal out of here!"

"Good," said Eddie. "I can still make the second half of the game."

"Oh. Un-unh," said Raven, shaking her head. "You're not making *nothing* until this goat makes with my wristbands!"

"Guys, we have a problem," Chelsea called from the grass.

Raven rolled her eyes. "Chels, you just noticed that?"

"No," Chelsea said. Her voice was serious. "Something's wrong with Gomez."

Everyone realized the little goat was no longer standing. He was lying on his side, panting. Chelsea knelt down next to him.

"Maybe he's just tired from tearing stuff up," Cory suggested.

"No, it's serious." She felt his nose. "He's sick. His nose is dry and his eyes look watery."

Raven crouched down. "Oh, Chelsea's right. He doesn't look so good. What do you think's wrong with him?"

Chelsea frowned in thought. "Maybe it's something he ate."

Right, thought Raven, that narrows it down. "He ate *everything*."

Eddie scratched his head. "Well, what do we do?"

Chelsea rose and faced Raven's parents. "Mr. and Mrs. B, I want you to call Dr. Carrington. He's the best vet in town. Tell him it's Chelsea and that we have a goat down."

She turned to Raven, Cory, and Eddie. "Rae, you get some blankets. Cory, I need an ice bag. Eddie, get a baby bottle with warm milk. *Stat!*"

Everyone was silent for a long moment. They simply stood there, staring at Chelsea in disbelief.

Dang, thought Raven, my flaky friend's turned into Dr. Chelsea, Medicine Woman. What's up with that?!

"Yeah, I know," Chelsea told them. "It's me. Now move! Move! Move!" She slapped her leg. "Let's go! Let's go!"

Suddenly, everyone was in motion, doing

exactly what Chelsea commanded. After they all ran off, she sat down with her sick little friend.

"Hey, don't worry, Gomez," she cooed. "We're going to get through this."

Chapter Five

An hour later, Camp Gomez had become Goat General Hospital. Raven sat cross-legged on the grass, holding Gomez in a purple blanket. Eddie fed him warm milk from a baby bottle. And Chelsea stroked his head and monitored his temperature.

"Hang in there, little fella," Chelsea cooed. "You know what? You're doing okay. You're with your friends now."

"Yeah, we got your furry little back," said Eddie. He tilted the baby bottle higher as Gomez slurped away. "Chelsea, am I doing okay?"

Chelsea nodded. "Yeah, make sure you hold the bottle *upright*, y'know? So he doesn't suck in any air. Trust me, you do *not* want to burp a goat."

"Hey, guys!" Raven's dad called. He came out of the house and strode across the grass. "I just reached the vet on his cell phone. He was at the football game."

"Oh, Dad, what did he say?" Raven asked.

Mr. Baxter sighed. "He said Bayside's down forty-two to nothing."

"Oh, man!" Eddie cried.

"*Dad*," said Raven, "what did he say about the *goat*?"

"Oh, yeah, right!" said Mr. Baxter. "Well, he said Chelsea should just keep doing what she's doing and to check in with him later."

"Baaaa, baaaa," bleated Gomez.

Raven, Eddie, and Chelsea went back to comforting their sick little friend. That's when Eddie noticed something coming from his back end.

"*Hello.* Looks like it's Christmas," he said, "'cause Gomez just left us a little present."

Raven and Chelsea glanced behind the goat.

"Oh, my wristbands!" Raven said excitedly. "*Eww* and something else," she added, holding her nose.

With a little bleat, Gomez moved to stand.

"Hey, he's up!" Eddie cried. He stroked the little goat's bearded chin. "Attaboy!"

"Look at that," said Chelsea. "His eyes are clear, and his nose is moist. I think he's feeling better."

"Guys, we did it!" Raven cried. "We fixed the goat!" She gave high fives to Eddie and Chelsea.

A few moments later, Raven's mom walked across the yard. "Guys, your limo's waiting," she called. "Oh, and I explained the goat situation to the driver. He said you'll have brand-new wristbands when you get to the show."

"Good," said Raven. "'Cause that was *not* going to match the color of my outfit." Her face pruned up at the sad, smelly state of her wristbands.

"Actually, Rae," Chelsea said apologetically, "I'm going to hang here with Gomez and make sure everything's okay. Why don't you just take your mom to the concert?"

Mrs. Baxter looked thunderstruck. "Really? Me, Rae, Boyz 'N Motion?!"

Raven's mother squealed like a teenager. She bent over, swung out her hip and began doing a sort of mixing-bowl motion with her upper body.

Dang, thought Raven with a shudder. Those tired moves are really sad—and possibly dangerous!

"Mom, Mom, Mom!" she cried, rushing over to stop the woman from hurting herself.

"What, honey?" asked Mrs. Baxter.

"If you do that at the concert, I don't *know* you."

"Hey, you guys," Eddie interrupted. "Do you mind dropping me off at the game? I'm going to look the team *straight* in the eye and tell them the truth."

"The *truth*?" Raven repeated.

He shrugged. "The goat ran away."

Beep-beep! Beep-beep!

The limo driver was honking out front.

"Go, go, go," urged Chelsea. "You guys are going to be late. Go, go."

Raven, Eddie, and Mrs. Baxter nodded. They petted Gomez one last time, said good-bye to Chelsea, and headed into the house.

"It's going to be okay," Chelsea told the little goat. "I'm not going to leave you. . . ."

Raven overheard Chelsea as she followed Eddie and her mom into the house. And she knew what she had to do.

"Mom?" Raven called.

Mrs. Baxter didn't hear her daughter. She was so psyched about going to the Boyz 'N Motion concert, she'd actually started performing the pop group's trademark song.

"Boyz!" *Stomp!* "We are the Boyz 'N Motion." *Clap!* "We give you our devotion. Boyz!" *Stomp!* "We are the Boyz 'N Motion." *Clap!* "We give you our—"

"Mom, hold up!" Raven cried.

Mrs. Baxter finally halted her Mama 'N Motion.

"Um . . ." said Raven. "You wouldn't mind if I didn't go to the concert with you, right?"

"Why?" Mrs. Baxter asked worriedly. "What's wrong?"

"Well, I just . . ." Raven shrugged. "I want to hang here with Chelsea. You can go with Dad, right?"

Mrs. Baxter nodded. "All right . . ." she said. Then she shrugged and headed toward the living room to find her husband. "I just hope he doesn't *embarrass* me."

Eddie touched Raven's shoulder. "Rae, what happened? Why aren't you going to the concert?"

Raven sighed and confessed. "Dang goat got to me."

Eddie leaned on the kitchen counter. "Yeah, he got to me, too. Why'd he have to be so cute?"

"And cuddly!" Raven added. "Eddie, you know what the scariest part is?"

Eddie could already guess. "We're starting to think like Chelsea?"

Raven nodded. "Maybe it's not such a bad thing."

When it came to brains, Chelsea was no mental giant. But no one had a bigger heart than Raven's best girlfriend. For that, Raven had to give Chelsea props.

"C'mon," she told Eddie.

The two of them walked back into the Baxters' yard. Chelsea didn't notice them returning. She was still sitting on the grass, comforting Gomez.

"Hey, I've got a little secret to tell you," she cooed to the goat. "You know how I was acting all brave and everything? Well, you had me pretty scared."

"But he's okay now. Aren't you, boy?" Raven said.

"Yeah," said Eddie, "and we're going to tell you all about life on the farm."

Chelsea turned, surprised to see her best friends hadn't left yet. "You *guys* . . ." she said as they sat down next to her and Gomez. "What are you doing here? What about the concert? And the game?"

Raven shrugged. "The Boyz will always be in motion."

Eddie nodded. "And I can lie to the team tomorrow."

"Yeah, besides," said Raven, "how often can we sit next to our best friend and our new favorite goat?"

"Baaaaaaaaaa!" Gomez bleated.

Eddie glanced behind the ex–Jefferson mascot. "Hey, it's Christmas again!"

Raven pointed at the grass. In the middle of the goat's stinky pile was a familiar shimmer of silver metal. "You guys, it's my cell phone. *Hey.*" She'd been wondering where her phone had disappeared to!

Just then, the phone began to jingle. *Briing! Briing! Briing!*

Raven, Eddie, and Chelsea all stared at the jingling pile of stink. Raven shuddered. "Y'all want to get that?" she desperately asked her peeps.

Eddie and Chelsea exchanged grossed-out glances. "Nope! Un-unh! No way!" they said together.

The next day at school, Raven and Eddie were chatting near their lockers when Chelsea rushed up to them.

"Hey, hey, hey, you guys," she said. "I just got a report from the farm."

The night before, Chelsea's vet friend had picked up Gomez after the football game and took him to a farm outside the city.

"You'll be very happy to know Gomez had a comfortable night and that he's liked and accepted by all his fellow goats," Chelsea proclaimed.

"Chels, that is wonderful," said Raven. "I'm going to miss that beardy-chin and goaty-breath little thing!"

"Yeah," said Eddie. "I'm glad the little

homey Gomez is chillin'. But I talked to the principal, and he says that since I was the one that stole the goat, I've got to come up with a new mascot for Jefferson."

All of a sudden, Raven felt a tingling over her entire body. And she knew what that meant. Eddie's words were sending her into a psychic trance!

Through her eye
The vision runs
Flash of future
Here it comes—

Okay, what am I seeing? Looks like the Jefferson football stadium. And, man, is it packed! I guess it's game day. The cheerleaders are cheering, the players are playing, and the fans in the stands are waving their hands.

Oh, look! The cheerleaders are about to

lead the crowd in an organized cheer. They're shaking their red-and-white Patriots pom-poms, kicking high, and clapping loud. Well, why not? At least their team knows how to score a touchdown.

Hey, look at that! Some student is running onto the field in a goat costume. The crowd's going wild. Looks like Jefferson's got themselves a brand-new school mascot after all. And, dang! The kids really love him!

I wonder who he is?

Hey, the guy in the goat suit is finally turning around. Now I can see his face.

Oh, snap! It's Eddie!

Eddie Thomas is the new Jefferson mascot?!

"Go, Jefferson!" Eddie yells. Now he's bending down and bleating, just like Gomez.

"Beaaaaaaat Bayside!"

As Raven came out of her vision, she shook her head clear and shuddered.

Eddie stared at her, waiting to hear about her glimpse of the future. "What is it, Rae? Did you see something about Jefferson? Did I find them a new mascot?"

"Uh, Eddie," she said, putting a hand on her homeboy's shoulder. "I've got some *baaaaaaad* news."

Part Two

"What goat?" asked Chelsea.

"He A-T-E your wristbands?" Mrs. Baxter asked.

"Cory, you have been playing that game for hours," Mrs. Baxter said.

"I just got a report from the farm," Chelsea said. "Gomez had a comfortable night and he's liked and accepted by all his fellow goats."

"I did the coolest thing," Eddie said.

"We couldn't beat 'em if we stole the whole team," said Raven.

"Your stinkin' goat ain't in there," Raven said.

"It's the Boyz 'N Motion wristbands!" Raven said.

"Since we're keepin' it real, let's keep
it real clean," said Mrs. Baxter.

"Order for the Boyz! Two eggs, over easy.
Side of turkey bacon, crisp. And do not
let them touch," said Mrs. Baxter.

"They don't have my back, after all,"
Raven told her parents.

"Check it out, no Boyz, just Baxter
and her crew," said Bianca.

Part Two

"Oh, snap," Raven murmured to herself,
"no autographs?"

"It would be an honor to have you stay for dinner,"
Mrs. Baxter told Boyz 'N Motion.

"We have plenty of room. Mom, Dad, please tell them that they would not be putting us out," said Raven.

"For your information, the Boyz are my boys. They will do anything for me," snapped Raven.

Chapter One

"**O**kay, guys, listen up!" called Mr. Baxter.

Raven's dad strode out of his restaurant's kitchen wearing a white chef's jacket and a serious expression. The waiters and waitresses gathered around him in the empty dining room.

"As you know," he began, "the world-famous band Boyz 'N Motion are coming down here today to the Chill Grill."

Standing in the back of the group, Raven Baxter couldn't stop herself. "Aaaaaaaaah!" she screamed.

The waiters and waitresses covered their ears, and Mr. Baxter shot his daughter a silencing look. There was a reason he'd named his restaurant Chill Grill, and tonight he expected his daughter to remember the "chill" part!

That wouldn't be easy for Raven. She was about to meet Boyz 'N Motion *live* and *in person*! The whole thing was off the hook!

Around her, the restaurant's tables were completely empty. The Chill Grill's regular customers were being turned away with a sign on the door that read: CLOSED FOR A PRIVATE PARTY. And Raven couldn't wait to get that party started!

"Anyway," Mr. Baxter continued, "they're in town doing a music video, and their people called and asked for a quiet dinner away from autographs—"

"Oh, snap," Raven murmured to herself, "no autographs?"

Mr. Baxter threw his daughter a warning look, and she quickly stuffed her autograph book back into her handbag.

"And away from *cameras*," Mr. Baxter added.

"Dang, not even one little picture?" Raven whispered. But her dad's stern stare forced her to put away her camera, too.

"Or screaming fans," Mr. Baxter finished.

This one was the hardest of all. Raven felt another scream building inside her. She squeezed her eyes shut, but she couldn't stop it. Up, up, up it came, until finally: "Aaaaaaaaaaaah!"

Her father folded his arms and waited for an explanation. Raven shrugged apologetically. "That one had a mind of its own," she said.

Just then, the front door opened, and Raven nearly lost it again when she saw who was strutting through. The three hottest dudes in pop music entered the Chill Grill wearing the coolest attitudes.

"Dad," Raven whispered, her voice quivering, "it's Tre, JJ, and Ricky!"

Tre was the baddest of the group, with his loose walk and tight do rag. JJ was the sweetest, with his surfer-dude hair and dimpled smile. And Ricky was the smoothest, with his dark eyes and slick style.

The three boys checked out the restaurant as they walked toward a table. When they went past Raven, she actually trembled. Reaching out a hand, she brushed their clothing.

"How you doin'?" she chirped excitedly.

The boys nodded at Raven. They sat down at a table, and a waiter moved toward them.

"I *touched* them," Raven whispered to her father. "Dad, *thank you* for having them. And thank you for having *me!*"

Mr. Baxter smiled as he pried Raven's clenched fingers off his chef's jacket. "Sweetheart, you're welcome. And thank *you* for keeping it a *secret.*"

Raven's bubbly grin suddenly went flat. "Keeping it a . . . huh?"

Mr. Baxter frowned. He read his daughter's guilty face like a large-print menu. "Rae . . . you've been bragging about this at school, haven't you?"

Raven gulped. "Dad, come on. I was just, you know, talking to some of the peeps about the situation, and they were lingering on my every word. But they did all promise to keep it on the down-low."

Mr. Baxter was about to ask just how "down low" her friends were going to keep it, but he didn't have a chance. The restaurant's front door burst open. Chelsea Daniels rushed into the middle of the dining room. Fixing her gaze on Tre, JJ, and Ricky, she screamed. "Boyz 'N Motion!"

Raven was horrified. "Chels, no! Don't, don't!"

But it was too late. The damage was done. Raven's gossip about the Boyz' little dinner-time visit had spread far and wide. Not only did Chelsea have a crazed look in her eyes, so did the mob of squealing females, bursting into the restaurant right behind her.

"Get 'em!" Chelsea cried to her pop-star-hunting posse. And the squealing teens rushed the Boyz' table.

Mr. Baxter stepped between his three special customers and their rioting fans. "All right," he shouted, "everybody calm—"

The mob rolled right over Raven's father!

Now the Boyz 'N Motion actually *were* in motion. They jumped to their feet and began to run around the dining room. But they couldn't find an exit! They didn't know where to go!

Oh, snap, Raven thought, since I'm the one who caused this thing, I'd better step up.

"Boyz, follow me!" she yelled over the screaming girls.

Tre, JJ, and Ricky followed Raven through the doors to the kitchen. The mob was right on their heels!

"C'mon!" Raven urged, waving them into the restaurant's storeroom. Once Tre, JJ, and Ricky were safely inside, Raven slammed the door and locked it.

"Boyz! Boyz! Boyz!" the girls chanted as they pounded the door.

"Get out and stay out!" Raven yelled to her crazed classmates. Then she turned to the panic-stricken pop stars and smiled sweetly.

"How y'all doing?" she purred.

Chapter Two

A little later that evening, Raven waved the three famous singers through another door, the one to her own home.

"Hey, Mom?" she called, walking into the living room. "Can JJ, Ricky, and Tre stay for dinner?"

Mrs. Baxter was sitting on the sofa, helping Cory with his homework. "That's funny," she told Raven. "That's the same names as—"

Mrs. Baxter's tongue stopped working for a few seconds when the three international pop stars strutted into her living room.

"Boyz 'N Motion!" she shouted, leaping to her feet. "Oh! Oh! I love your songs!"

To prove it, Mrs. Baxter began performing

their biggest hit tune. "Boyz!" she cried with a booty shake. "We are the Boyz 'N Motion." *Clap!* "We nuh-nuh, nuh, nuh, nuh, nuh!"

Raven cringed. Her mother was so excited, she'd forgotten the words to the Boyz' number one song. Plus she was making their trademark steps look more like a health club aerobics routine.

"Mom, Mom," Raven said, rushing over to end the embarrassment. "I know you're excited. I know! But we've got to take it *down*."

"But it's Boyz 'N Motion!" Mrs. Baxter squealed, bouncing on her heels.

"I know!" Raven cried. Then both she *and* her mother bit their fists to keep from screaming.

"But we've got to be cool," Raven mumbled around her hand.

Mrs. Baxter nodded. She knew Raven was right, and she did her best to compose herself.

"Sorry," she told the pop stars. "I'm Raven—"
She shook her head. "No, uh, I'm *Tanya*
Baxter," she corrected. "Raven's *mother*." Then
she pointed to the boy on the sofa. "This is my
son, Cory."

Raven's little brother barely looked up from
his notebook. "Hey," he said, lifting a pencil in
greeting.

Unlike his mother and sister, Cory Baxter
wasn't much of a Boyz 'N Motion fan. To him,
Tre, JJ, and Ricky were just three pretty dudes
in T-shirts, standing in the middle of his living
room.

One of those dudes stepped forward. "Well,
I'm Ricky," said the dark-haired boy with big
brown eyes and a heart-stopping smile. He
pointed to the lanky guy with the little goatee
and bad-boy do rag. "This is Tre."

"'Sup?" said Tre with a wave.

Then Ricky pointed to the shaggy-haired

blond boy with the baseball cap. "And this is JJ."

JJ flashed his dimpled, surfer-dude smile. "It's actually JJJ," he noted, "with the third J . . . *silent.*"

"Well, it would be an *honor* to have you stay for dinner," said Mrs. Baxter. But she wondered why the boys weren't eating at the Chill Grill. "Did something happen at the restaurant?"

"Crazed fans. Near riot. Typical Wednesday," Tre informed her with a weary sigh.

Ricky nodded. "It's lucky Raven got us out that storeroom window."

"Dude," said Tre, "we can't even go back to our hotel." He moved to the front door and peeked out the glass, just to make sure they weren't being followed. "*Someone* found out we were in town and spread it around."

Mrs. Baxter shook her head. "Who would do such a thing?"

Raven tensed. "Hey, hey, hey, people!" she cried, stopping them before they could figure it out. "Okay, let's not play the blame game, all right? Whoever did it probably had a simple lapse in judgment."

"Or a big mouth," said Cory, shooting a suspicious glance his big sister's way.

Raven grimaced. Clearly, the little worm thinks I'm guilty, she thought. Well, he better keep his piehole shut, or I'll superglue it that way *permanently*!

Mrs. Baxter smiled sympathetically at the Boyz. "It must be tough to be famous."

Tre nodded. "Like we said in our smash hit, 'Fame Can Be A Pain.'" He glanced at JJ and Ricky. "Fame can be a pain!" they all sang in three-part harmony.

Biting their fists, Raven and her mom made strangled noises. Boyz 'N Motion had just sung! In three-part harmony! In their own home! They could barely contain their excited screams.

Forcing herself to chill, Raven removed her fist from her mouth. *Ouch!* This time she'd bit down a little too hard on the ol' knuckles.

"I feel your pain," she assured the Boyz. "Come sit . . ."

The boys collapsed on the Baxters' sofa. "It's crazy out there, Rae. Everybody wants a piece of us," said Tre.

Ricky nodded. "Check it out. I wiped my face with a paper towel, and the next day it was on the Internet selling for major loot!"

"Really?" said Cory.

These pretty-boy pop singers had finally said something that interested him. Of course, as a wannabe tycoon, the phrase "major loot" was always music to his ears.

"I'm sure you boys are hungry," Mrs. Baxter said. She invited them into her kitchen, and before long, the three singers were enjoying a tasty home-cooked meal.

"Is it good?" Cory asked Tre.

Sitting at the Baxters' kitchen table, Tre nodded enthusiastically. He couldn't speak because his mouth was full. He was gobbling down his fourth piece of fried chicken.

Like a pudgy vulture, Cory leaned closer to the pop star. "You're done with those chicken bones, right?"

Before Tre could answer, Cory plucked the greasy bones right out of his fingers and ran off to a corner of the kitchen. "Cha-ching," he whispered to himself as he dropped Tre's bones inside a plastic bag.

I can just see my Internet listing now, Cory thought, sealing the bag. *Bid on Boyz' Bones, Still Sticky with Stars' Saliva!*

"Who's ready for thirds?" asked Mrs. Baxter, carrying over a fresh platter of fried chicken.

The pop stars were grabbing up pieces before she'd even set the dish down.

Ricky bit into a crispy chicken leg and licked his lips. "Mrs. Baxter, we've been on tour for years. We haven't had a home-cooked meal like this since our first smash hit, 'Bye, Bye, Bye, Home Cookin'.'"

Once again, the Boyz broke into three-part harmony. "Bye, bye, bye, home cookin'!"

Raven nearly swooned. She couldn't believe the Boyz were singing again—and this time in her very own kitchen!

"Man," said Ricky, "I can't believe we've got to go back to that hotel, with all those screaming fans."

"Don't go!" Raven suddenly cried. "I mean . . ." she calmed herself. "Why? Why *should* you go?"

Since the Boyz had sat down, Raven had been soaking up their every move, every word, every chew, swallow, and napkin wipe. Spending time like this with Tre, JJ, and Ricky was like a dream come true. She couldn't bear to see it end! She *had* to think of a way to keep the Boyz in her house.

"You know what?" Raven said, tapping her cheek in thought. "Actually, I was thinking you guys should really just step back from this crazy life. Take a break. You know, try to be *normal* for a while."

"Oh, we don't want to put you out," said Ricky.

"Put us out?" Raven said. "*Please.* We have plenty of room. You would not be putting us out. Mom, Dad, please tell them that they would not be putting us out."

Mr. and Mrs. Baxter exchanged uncertain glances. Three unexpected house guests could be a lot of trouble. But Raven was determined.

"*Tell 'em!*" she shouted.

"Uh, it's no problem," her dad said uneasily.

"We'd love to have you," her mom added weakly.

Tre nodded. "Okay. We'll hang."

"Thank you, guys!" Ricky grinned at the Baxters. "And, Raven, if you ever need anything, *anything at all*, you name it. 'Cause the Boyz got your back."

Raven nearly had a stroke when Ricky, Tre, and JJ clenched their fists, tapped their hearts, and tossed her peace-out signs.

"They got my back," she whispered in awe, deciding this was possibly *the* best single moment of her entire life.

Chapter Three

The next morning at school, Raven felt as if *she* were the pop star. She'd barely opened her locker before every girl at Bayside mobbed her. They all wanted the 411 on the Boyz 'N Motion!

"What did they say? What did they do? Where did they go? What were they like? . . . *Tell* us!"

"People, people!" Chelsea shouted, clapping her hands. "Let *me* be the mob spokesperson, okay?"

Since all the girls knew Chelsea was Raven's best friend, they settled down and let her take over.

"Now, Raven," said Chelsea, putting a hand

on her shoulder, "after you went out the back door with the Boyz, where did you go?"

"Oh, everybody—" Raven began, then stopped herself. She wanted to tell them everything: that Tre, JJ, and Ricky loved her mama's fried chicken. That they sang in three-part harmony just for her. And right now, right this very minute, they were living as guests in her very own home! But Raven's bragging had messed things up for the Boyz once already. She didn't want that to happen again.

"Look," she finally told her panting classmates, "what *happens* between me and the Boyz, *stays* between me and the Boyz."

The girls whispered and murmured. Raven hadn't said much, but it was *enough*! She'd obviously spent some quality time with the three hottest boys in pop music!

As Raven gathered her books and headed down the hall to class, she thought the drama was over. But she thought wrong. The bad girls of Bayside were about to ruin her day.

Loca stepped in front of Raven, blocking her path. Loca crossed her arms. Then little priss Muffy moved forward and tossed her straight blond hair.

"Bianca feels that you don't even *know* the Boyz," Muffy said with a smirk.

"Bianca?" said Raven. "Where's Alana?"

For years, Alana had been Bayside's teen queen of mean. Loca and Muffy were part of her crew and made Raven's life miserable. As Eddie used to rap: *If somethin' mean's goin' down behind the scenes, you can bet it's from Alana and her gangsta-girl schemes.*

"Oh, I guess you haven't heard," Muffy told Raven. "Alana was so bad she got sent to military school."

Military school? "Yes!" Raven couldn't believe her luck. First the Boyz had her back, and now the wicked witch of Bayside would have to get off her broomstick and learn how to salute!

But Raven's triumph was short-lived.

"We run with *Bianca* now," Loca informed her.

Muffy nodded. "She's so bad she got kicked *out* of military school."

"Oh, snap . . ." Raven groaned. So much for good news. On the other hand, she thought, how bad could Bianca be?

"Hey!" barked a voice from down the hall.

A Latina girl with curly brown hair and a superdiva attitude sashayed right up to Raven. Loca and Muffy immediately stepped up to back her.

Raven gulped. I guess this is the new queen bee, she thought. "Hey, hey . . . Hi, Bianca. Uh, before we get off on the wrong foot—"

"Too late," Bianca declared. Filing her nails,

she looked Raven up and down. "I don't like you already," she sneered.

Muffy's head bobbed. "Oh, oh, and um, Bianca also doesn't like your *shoes*."

"What?" said Chelsea, stepping up to defend her best friend. "She never said anything about Raven's shoes."

"She was gettin' to it," said Loca. Then the giant girl bent down to get into Chelsea's face. "You got a problem with that?"

Chelsea gulped at the sheer size of Loca's head. "No, no, I don't," she squeaked like a terrorized mouse. "Actually, I don't like her shoes, either."

"Hey!" said Raven. "What have y'all got against my shoes!"

Bianca snapped her fingers. "Come on, Baxter, the Boyz would never waste their time with *you*."

"Yes, they would," Raven insisted. "The Boyz got my back."

"Nuh-uh," said Bianca, working her head.

"Uh-huh," said Raven, working it right back.

Bianca waved her nail file. "Yeah, and I was partyin' with Beyoncé last night."

"Oh, my gosh, that is *so* cool," said Chelsea, her eyes wide with awe. "Is she nice?"

Raven gritted her teeth. "Chels, she doesn't know Beyoncé."

Chelsea rolled her eyes. "Rae, then why was she *partying* with her, *hello?*"

Bianca smirked. "Just admit it, Baxter, you're *lying.*"

"Nuh-uh!" said Raven.

"Uh-huh!" said Bianca.

A minute ago, Raven had been annoyed, but now she wasn't playing. *No* one, she thought, least of all this girl with an *I'm-all-that* attitude, is going to call me a liar!

"For your information, okay, the Boyz are

my boys, okay," said Raven. "They will do *any-thing* for me. They got my back, like I said."

"Okay," said Bianca, coolly propping one hip. "Then make 'em sing at the school's music festival tonight."

"Done," said Raven.

Bianca blinked. For a second, she was so surprised that Raven had agreed, she didn't know what to say.

"Well, you know what?" she finally snapped. "I'll believe it when I see it."

Muffy pursed her lips and nodded. "When Bianca sees it, she'll believe it."

Tossing her brown curls, Bianca strode off. Muffy hurried to catch up. But Loca hung back. She bent down toward Raven and whispered, "Could you get me an autograph?"

"Loca!" Bianca barked from down the hall.

Loca quickly straightened to her full height. "I better not catch you in those shoes again!"

she loudly warned Raven in her tough voice. Then she threw Raven a secret wink and ran off to join her crew.

"Rae, this is so cool!" Chelsea gushed. "When the Boyz show up at that music festival tonight, the whole school's going to love you!"

"I know," said Raven. And that's when she felt it—the familiar tingling. The psychic energy electrified her body and sped through her mind. For a split second, Raven's whole world seemed to freeze in time. . . .

**Through her eye
The vision runs
Flash of future
Here it comes—**

Check it out! It's the school music festival. Everyone's packed into Bayside's auditorium.

I can see a whole lot of familiar faces—there's Kaneesha, Amber, and Marisol. And I see smug Bianca's here with her Nasty Girls crew, too. Ugh.

Wait! Something's happening. The audience seems really angry and upset for some reason. They're booing and yelling. They're throwing wrappers and popcorn and trash at the stage!

Whoa, they're acting like a total mob now. And they're beginning to chant. But I can hardly make out what they're saying. . . .

Oh, wait! It's clear now—

"We hate Raven! We hate Raven!"

As Raven came out of her psychic trance, she felt a little sick.

"Raven, what is it?" asked Chelsea. "Did you just have a vision?"

"Yeah," said Raven.

If her vision of the future turned out to be true, then her dreamy experience with the Boyz was about to turn into a nightmare. Unless . . .

"Chels? Do you know if there's anyone *else* in this school named *Raven*?"

Chapter Four

Later that afternoon, Mrs. Baxter walked out of the kitchen with a laundry basket under her arm. Shaking her head, she took in the messed-up state of her beautiful living room.

Clothing was carelessly thrown over lamps, tables, and chairs. Bags of chips and snack wrappers were tossed all over the floor, and cans of soda had left rings on her polished side tables.

The Boyz were in here, too, but none of them were even close to being in motion. Sprawled across the furniture, they'd been snoring away for half the day!

As Mrs. Baxter began picking up their dirty laundry, she startled Ricky awake. He rolled over in the cushioned window seat and fell to the floor.

Thump!

"Hey, you're up," said Mrs. Baxter. "Great."

"What time is it?" Ricky asked, rubbing his big brown eyes.

"Three thirty," Mrs. Baxter told him.

On the couch, JJ yawned and scratched his shaggy blond head. "Mrs. B, is it the *dark* three thirty or the *sunny* one?"

"The sunny one, dear," she said.

"Righteous," he said and put his head back down on the sofa pillow.

Tre nodded on the overstuffed armchair. "Yo, Mrs. B., we really appreciate you letting us chill here. It feels great being in a *real* home."

"With a *real* family," Ricky added, smiling at Cory as he walked into the room.

Mrs. Baxter folded her arms. She could

believe the Boyz appreciated being in a *real* home. But they'd obviously forgotten that *real* homes didn't come with *real* armies of hotel maids.

"Since we're keepin' it real, let's keep it real *clean*," she advised them. Then she bent over and began picking up scattered snack wrappers, chip bags, and empty soda cans.

"Oh, Mother, please! Allow me!" Cory cried, rushing up to her with a plastic bag. He took all of the trash she'd collected and stuffed it inside. Then he began collecting the rest— empty juice boxes, straws, used napkins.

Mrs. Baxter eyed her young son with suspicion. It wasn't like Cory to volunteer for clean-up duty. He had to be up to something. But what?

"Cha-ching . . . cha-ching . . ." Cory whispered to himself with every piece of trash he collected. Then he noticed JJ shifting on the couch. The boy's sock-covered feet were propped up high on the sofa's back cushion.

Wow, Cory thought, I'll bet I could get a fortune on the Internet for a single stinky JJ sock!

A second later, he was plucking the sock off JJ's foot and running up the stairs with his pop-star treasure.

Mrs. Baxter scratched her head. She didn't know *what* Cory was doing, but she didn't stop him. Cleaning up after these three internationally famous slobs was going to be a full-time job, and she could use all the help she could get!

Upstairs, Cory rushed into his bedroom and started sorting the items in his plastic bag. Across the room, Cory's friend William was sitting at the desk, typing away on Cory's laptop.

"What did you get this time?" William asked.

Cory had joined forces with his brainy little friend to run their new Internet business: Boyz 'N Motion—Trash 4 U!

"Check this out!" Cory showed William his latest scores: JJ's stinky sock, Ricky's empty bag of chips . . . "And look!" Cory cried. "Tre's freshly sucked straws. Man, these have got to be worth serious bucks on the Internet!"

"Tell me about it," said William. "We just got twenty dollars for Tre's gravy-stained napkin. But according to my research, we can get big money for a lock of their hair."

Cory's eyes brightened. He'd just heard his two favorite words: "big money."

With a devious smile, Cory picked up a pair of scissors. From what he could see, the three pretty-boy stars could carry a tune, but they weren't all that bright. So how hard would it be to convince one of them to give up a little hair?

With glee, Cory worked the scissors in his hand. The *snip, snip, snip* sounded sweeter than three-part harmony!

While Cory was upstairs making money, his father was in the kitchen making breakfast.

Even though it was three thirty in the afternoon, the pop stars had just woken up. And they expected the first meal of the day—*their* way.

"Order for the Boyz," Mrs. Baxter told her husband as she walked in from the living room. "Two eggs, over easy. Side of *turkey* bacon, *crisp*. And *do not* let them touch."

Mr. Baxter's brow wrinkled. "Why?"

Mrs. Baxter rolled her eyes. "The Boyz do not like their foods to touch."

"I've got to go back to my restaurant," said Mr. Baxter in exasperation.

"Mom!" called Raven, rushing in through the back door. "Are the Boyz still here?!"

Mrs. Baxter jerked her thumb toward the mess she'd just left. "They're in the living room, thinking up ways to work my nerves."

"Good," said Raven, sighing with relief. "'Cause Bianca was at school. And she was, like, 'You don't know the Boyz.' And I was, like, 'Uh-huh.' And she was, like, 'Nuh-uh.' And I was, like, *'Uh-huh!'* And she was, like, *'Nuh-uh!'* And I was, like, 'Uh—'"

"Rae!" Mr. Baxter interrupted. "*Short* version."

Raven shrugged. "Basically, I promised that the Boyz would perform at school tonight."

"Nuh-uh!" Mrs. Baxter cried.

"Uh-huh!" Raven replied. "And, Mom, if they *don't*, everybody's going to *hate* me!"

Raven's vision of the future had her buggin'. If she didn't get the Boyz to perform, her classmates would be chanting a whole new Bayside cheer: *We hate Raven! We hate Raven!*

Chelsea was so freaked, she'd actually checked the student roster in the principal's office. But there was no other "Raven" in the house! Raven's vision was about Raven *Baxter*. No doubt.

"Rae, you see?" scolded her father. "*This* is what happens when you go around bragging!"

"You know what?" said Raven. "We shouldn't even be worrying about all this. Because the Boyz said they got my back."

With a deep breath, Raven confidently strode forward, right into the living room. At the sight of the megamess, she froze and stepped back.

Oh, snap, she thought, my mama wasn't kidding. These major stars are major slobs!

Shaking it off, Raven pressed ahead. She brightly greeted the Boyz and then asked them for that one little ol' favor. Would they sing at her school's music festival?

The Boyz glanced at each other and gave her their answer.

"No?" Raven repeated in shock. "But I thought you had my back?!"

Ricky shrugged. "Hey, if you had asked us yesterday, we would have said what we say in our smash hit, 'Yes! In a Heartbeat.'"

"Yes! In a heartbeat!" the three Boyz sang.

Raven tried not to panic. "I just don't understand. Why can't you just sing *one* song?"

"Sorry," Ricky said. "The Boyz have decided to get out of show business."

Raven's jaw dropped. "Why would you do something stupid like that?!"

"You told us to," JJ reminded her.

"No, I didn't, JJ, okay?" said Raven defensively. "I said *stay for dinner.*"

Tre shook his head. "You said we need to

step back from this crazy life, take a break. Try to be normal."

Raven was buggin'. This was unreal. She had to think fast to change their minds. "Well, what about . . . what about your smash hit?" she told them. "What about 'Normal Ain't Cool?'"

The Boyz stared at Raven for a second, as if they couldn't remember the song.

"Normal ain't cool!" she sang for them.

The Boyz nodded. *"Normal ain't cool,"* they tried to sing. But they couldn't find a key, and their harmonies stunk.

"Hey, hey!" Ricky cried, realizing why they couldn't sing the song. "That's not one of ours! You just made that up!"

"Okay, okay, you got me," Raven admitted. "But I was trying to make a point. You can't quit."

"Hey, we already did," said Ricky. Then he

tossed her a grin. "Thanks to you, we've never been happier."

JJ nodded in agreement. But Tre grunted. Clearly, he was *un*happy.

For a second, Raven thought she had a chance. "Maybe Tre disagrees with his homeys," she whispered to herself in desperation. "Maybe he'll help me convince his co-stars to go back into showbiz."

But Tre's unhappiness had nothing to do with giving up singing. Meeting Raven's eyes, he lifted up his breakfast plate. "Can you give this back to your mom?" he said with a shudder. "The turkey bacon's *touching* the eggs."

Raven silently took the plate. Feeling defeated, betrayed, and a little bit angry at herself for believing the Boyz in the first place, she trudged back into the kitchen.

"How'd it go?" Mrs. Baxter asked.

Raven shrugged. "They don't have my back after all. . . ."

Mr. and Mrs. Baxter exchanged unhappy glances. Then Raven handed her father Prince Tre's breakfast plate.

"What's this?" he asked.

Raven rolled her eyes and sighed. "Food's touching."

Chapter Five

Raven felt a little queasy as she entered the school's auditorium. It was packed, of course. The music festival always got a good turnout. But the word had spread about her promise to bring the Boyz 'N Motion to the Bayside stage, and the event had completely sold out.

At this late hour, the audience had already seen most of the student performers: four bands, two rappers, and three solo singers. Onstage now was the last act of the evening, Bianca's Posse.

Bianca was the star of the girl group. Loca and Muffy were her backup singers. Behind the three girls, a DJ spun a driving beat.

Raven hated to admit it, but Bianca and her

crew looked tight. They had a kickin' routine and performed their steps with precision as they sang . . .

> *Bianca says run. You run!*
> *Bianca says hide. You hide!*
> *Bianca says stop. You stop!*
> *Bianca says go. You go!*
> *Bianca says jump. You say, how high?*
> *How hi-hi-hi-hi-hi-*
> *eeeee-iiiiiiiiigh?*

When the girls struck a final pose, the crowd applauded, and Raven held her breath. There were no more student acts scheduled. It was time for the music festival's grand finale—and Raven knew what that meant!

Bianca's posse was still onstage, taking their bows. As the applause died down, Muffy stepped forward with the microphone in hand.

"Thank you!" she told the audience. "And big ups to MC Feldman!"

The DJ behind her waved.

"Okay, now," Muffy continued, "I know you're all excited about Boyz 'N Motion visiting Bayside—"

The audience cheered, and all the girls screamed. When the noise finally subsided, Muffy told them, "But as Bianca predicted, the Boyz are *not* here."

Now disappointed murmurs buzzed through the crowd. In the back of the auditorium, Raven shifted nervously.

"I hate to mention names," Muffy continued with a smirk, "but Raven Baxter—"

"That's *Raven Baxter*," Bianca loudly repeated, grabbing hold of the mic.

"—has let us all down," Muffy continued, pulling the mic back. "She's not even here to apologize. Must be too embarrassed. Now if you'll all just exit in an orderly fashion . . ."

Muffy waited for the crowd to leave, but nobody moved. That's when Loca stepped forward and asked them to leave, *her* way.

"GET OUT!"

That did it. Everyone jumped up, ready to head for the door. But Raven refused to give up without a fight!

"No!" she shouted, moving down the auditorium's main aisle. "Everybody! Stay where you are!"

Bianca turned to Raven and sneered. "I hope you brought the Boyz with you."

"Well, Bianca," Raven replied loudly, "let's just say that in a couple of minutes, *everybody's* going to see a show that they'll never forget!"

The hopeful audience quickly took their seats again. An electric murmur raced through the rows.

Raven grinned at the crowd. "Make some noise!"

The crowd cheered, the girls screamed, and Bianca, Muffy, and Loca shared a skeptical look.

Here we go, thought Raven, feeling a little nervous as she darted backstage. Time for my Boyz to get *'N Motion*!

Meanwhile, back at Raven's house, Cory was on a quest for some high-end Internet merchandise: JJ's blond hair.

"Mr. Guillermo will give you a whole new look," Cory promised JJ, leading him upstairs. "He's the hottest hairstylist in the world."

JJ nodded as he followed Cory down the hall and into his room. It didn't occur to JJ to ask why a world-famous hairstylist was operating his salon in a little boy's bedroom.

"*Ciao!*" said William, bursting out of Cory's closet.

William had really gotten into the whole "Guillermo" act. He'd even agreed to wear one of Raven's cowboy hats with a ponytail sticking out of the back!

"There he is," Cory told JJ.

JJ scratched his shaggy head. "He's just a kid."

Cory nodded. "A kid genius."

Cory pushed JJ toward the "beauty station," which was really just a chair pulled up to Cory's cleared-off yellow desk. On the desk sat a pair of scissors, a hair dryer, a hand mirror, and a bunch of Mrs. Baxter's hair products.

JJ sat in the chair, and Cory draped a smock around his neck. Then William turned on the blow-dryer and gave JJ's hair a couple of fluffs.

"Is this going to take long?" JJ asked.

"Oh, no, no, no," said William.

William picked up the scissors and cut off a chunk of JJ's hair. Cory held open the little plastic bag and the hair dropped right into it.

"Voilà!" said William.

"You're done," Cory declared.

"That's it?" JJ asked.

Cory nodded as William doused him with a cloud of hair spray.

"That's it. *Arrivederci!*" said William, bidding him good-bye in Italian.

JJ picked up the hand mirror. "It doesn't even look like I got a haircut."

"I told you he was a genius!" said Cory, pulling the smock off JJ.

JJ nodded and smiled at his reflection in the mirror. "Righteous."

Cory snatched the mirror back and hustled JJ out of the chair. "Yeah, thank you! Come again!" Cory said. He pushed JJ out the door. Then he turned to William and shook the hair inside the bag.

Both boys pumped their arms. "Cha-ching!" they cried.

On his way down from Cory's salon, JJ noticed Mrs. Baxter coming in from the kitchen.

"Mrs. B," he called as she bent over to pick up some new trash, "check out the new haircut!" He spun around, modeling his hair.

"Doesn't look like you got one," said Mrs. Baxter.

JJ nodded knowingly. "That's the genius."

"Right. Okay, Boyz, dinner's ready," she called.

Ricky and Tre didn't move. They were sitting in front of the TV, intensely playing a video game.

"Not now, Mrs. B," Ricky told her. "We're full."

Mrs. Baxter wasn't surprised. An hour ago,

she'd cleaned this entire room. But once again the floor was littered with candy wrappers and empty snack bags.

"Yeah, yeah, yeah, yeah," Tre added. "We'll holla at you when we're hungry."

Mrs. Baxter didn't care for Tre's tone. "I'll holla at you now," she snapped. "Look at the mess in here!"

"Mrs. B, don't sweat it," said Tre. "Just have the maid clean it up."

"Hello, this is not a hotel," Mrs. Baxter reminded them. "I *am* the maid."

"Well, you're not doing such a hot job," said JJ, glancing around.

"Okay, that's it!" Mrs. Baxter threw up her hands. "I don't care how famous you are. All right, you want to be like regular people? Let me tell you something. Regular people have manners. They clean up after themselves. Oh, and when they make a *promise* to have somebody's back—" She tapped her chest and threw them a mock peace-out sign. "They *follow through* for them!"

The Boyz stared in shocked silence. They'd been international stars for years. Nobody had spoken to them like that in a long time.

Mrs. Baxter didn't care. She wasn't even waiting around for their response. She just stormed back toward the kitchen. On her way, she noticed Tre wearing a baseball cap over his blue do rag.

"No hat in my house!" she cried, ripping the cap off his head and throwing it into his lap.

The Boyz glanced at each other with guilty looks. Mrs. B was right, and they knew it. They'd been acting like selfish slobs. And they'd let down the girl who'd tried to help them most: Raven Baxter, their number one fan. The only question now was: what were they going to do about it?

Chapter Six

"**W**e want the Boyz! We want the Boyz!" chanted the Bayside crowd.

After Raven had disappeared backstage, the audience expected Boyz 'N Motion to come out and perform. But after fifteen minutes, not one boy was in motion!

Bianca elbowed Muffy. They had been waiting all day for this.

"People, people!" Muffy yelled, moving to stand in front of the stage. The audience stopped chanting, and Muffy cleared her throat.

"Okay. Well, I think we've all waited *long enough.*" Muffy scrunched up her face as if she were about to cry. "I'd like to thank the person who got our hopes up and then *crushed* them: Raven Baxter."

As Muffy brushed away invisible tears, Bianca and Loca stood up. "That's *Raven Baxter*," Bianca loudly repeated.

The audience decided Muffy was right. Raven had let them down. "Boo! Boo!" they shouted.

Just then, familiar music began to pulse through the auditorium speakers. The voices of Tre, JJ, and Ricky sang out.

"Boyz. We are the Boyz 'N Motion! We give you our devotion. Boyz. We are the Boyz 'N Motion! We give you our devotion. . . ."

It was the Boyz' trademark song! The boos turned to cheers as the curtain opened on three figures dancing with their backs to the audience.

Theatrical fog covered the stage. Lights were flashing, too, so it was hard to see the pop stars clearly. But their fans recognized the Boyz' familiar steps as their smash-hit tune continued to play. . . .

With all the fog and flashing lights, the crowd still couldn't see the Boyz very well. The three figures onstage were doing a lot of vogue poses, too, with hands in front of their faces. But the crowd could make out Ricky's short dark hair, JJ's blond hair and baseball cap, and Tre's do rag. And that was good enough for them.

The audience started rockin' out! Girls were screaming and guys were clapping. Shouts and cheers nearly drowned out the music.

Standing in the front row, Bianca folded her arms and turned to Muffy. "I can't believe Baxter got the Boyz here."

But Bianca was the only one who felt that way. Even Loca was impressed. "It's the Boyz!" she screamed and passed out. The tall girl fell backwards, knocking down the kids behind her like bowling pins.

Meanwhile, onstage, the three performers were doing their best to lip-synch to the recording. They couldn't actually *sing* the song, because they weren't really the world-famous pop stars. They were just impersonating them.

Using a short dark wig, Raven had dressed herself as Ricky. Chelsea was standing in for JJ, wearing a shaggy blond wig and baseball cap. And Eddie was playing the part of Tre with a tight blue do rag on his head and a small goatee glued to his chin.

So far, the flashing lights and fog machine were working like a charm. As long as the crowd couldn't see their faces, Raven figured she and her two best friends could get away with faking it.

But things soon became dicey onstage. Chelsea's long red hair was starting to fall out from under her blond wig. Raven danced over to her and tried to stuff it back into place.

Then Eddie ran into trouble. His sweat was loosening the glue on his Tre goatee. It was starting to fall off!

Still, the three friends kept dancing and pretending to sing.

From the front row, Bianca narrowed her eyes. "Something ain't right about those Boyz," she muttered. Sneaking backstage, she tried to get a closer look. But there was too much fog.

That's when she decided to clear the air. She noticed a fan in the wings, and she turned it on. In seconds, the fog onstage was blown clear.

Eddie got rattled and stepped on Raven's toe. She hopped around in pain. Then Eddie and Chelsea tried to cover by hopping around, too, as if it were part of the choreography.

The audience stopped cheering. They could see that something was definitely messed up with these Boyz.

Backstage, Bianca signaled to the DJ. He pulled out the cord to the soundboard. Suddenly, there was no more music.

The stage lights came up, and the audience finally saw who they were screaming and cheering and fainting for: Raven Baxter, Chelsea Daniels, and Eddie Thomas. Their own classmates were scamming them!

The three fake Boyz froze in place. Eddie kept moving his mouth, even though the music had stopped.

"Knick, knack, paddy-wack . . ." he sang off-key. He hadn't actually learned all the words to the Boyz 'N Motion song, so he'd been making them up all along.

The audience grumbled with simmering anger.

"Check it out!" Bianca told the crowd, rushing onto the stage. "No Boyz. Just Baxter and her crew!"

By now, Loca was back on her feet—and really angry, not to mention embarrassed. She shook her fist at Raven. "You made me faint for nothin'!" she yelled.

"Calm down!" Eddie yelled back.

As the crowd's grumbling grew louder, Bianca narrowed her eyes at Raven. "Let's see you lie your way out of this one, Baxter."

Raven took a deep breath and stepped up. "Okay, I did impersonate the Boyz," she confessed to the audience. "But I really do know them, you guys."

"Yeah, c'mon," said Chelsea. "In Raven's defense, the Boyz would have been here. It's just that Raven convinced them to quit show business forever."

The kids in the audience gasped.

"Thank you, Chelsea," muttered Raven. Then she made a decision. Her scam had been a big mistake. She should have been honest with her classmates from the start.

"Listen everybody, I'm sorry, okay?" she told them sincerely. "It's my fault for bragging and promising thc Boyz would be here tonight before I even asked them. So I hope you'll forgive me."

For a second, the audience was very quiet. And Raven thought they actually would forgive her. But then the groans and angry murmurs began. Bianca elbowed Muffy, and she started a chant that spread quickly through the crowd.

"*We hate Raven! We hate Raven! We hate Raven!*"

The trash came next. Popcorn, paper cups, balled-up candy wrappers were all thrown at the stage.

"Okay, okay," Raven cried, "I'll take that as a *no*."

Chelsea leaned close. "Well, at least your vision came true, Rae."

Raven rolled her eyes. "I can see that, Chels. *Thanks*."

Raven felt lower than low. All the kids had believed in her. Now they hated her. She'd bragged to them, scammed them, and let them down. For the rest of her years at Bayside, her classmates would never forget this night.

Just when Raven was about to cry, the Boyz' trademark music cranked up again. The audience cheered. Raven turned around and saw the reason. Striding onto the stage were the *real* JJ, Ricky, and Tre!

"What's up, Bayside?!" JJ shouted. Then he walked right over to Raven and gave her a *hug*!

Raven jumped up and down. "You came!" she squealed. "They came, everybody, they came!"

Loca's jaw dropped. "It really is the Boyz!"

Tre hugged Raven, too. Then Ricky put his arms around her and flashed his killer smile. "You know we had your back," he told her.

He turned to the audience. "And I hope you didn't mind that little trick we had our *friend* Raven and her crew play on you!"

"*Friend*," Raven repeated. She tossed a little payback smile Bianca's way. "Did you hear that?"

"That's right, we told you," Chelsea shouted.

The audience cheered.

"All right," Tre called, pacing the stage. "We're about to set it off. Let's do this! As we say in our smash hit, 'cause 'We are the Boyz 'N Motion . . .'"

This time the DJ had a *real* backup tape to play over the speakers, and the *real* Boyz began to sing and dance.

Once again, Loca fainted. But this time the kids behind her got a clue and moved away before she hit the floor.

Muffy and Bianca stared at the stage then exchanged unhappy looks. Raven had won. The Boyz were really here. And the crowd thought it was totally off the hook!

As the Boyz continued their song, they pulled Raven, Eddie, and Chelsea into the act. Even Muffy gave up the grump and began to get jiggy along with the crowd—until Bianca shot Muffy an angry look and made her stop dancing.

Raven didn't notice. She was too busy rockin' out with Tre, JJ, and Ricky. She couldn't believe it, but the Boyz really came through. They had her back, after all.

The next day, things were back to normal at Hotel Baxter. The Boyz had moved out, and

Mr. and Mrs. Baxter had cleaned up the mess they'd left behind.

Walking upstairs, they heard a funny fluttering sound coming from Cory's bedroom. They found their son sitting at his desk. His money-counting machine was going at full speed. He stuffed piles of bills in and out they came in neatly counted stacks.

"Every time I come in here he's counting money," said Mr. Baxter.

Mrs. Baxter walked up to her son. "Okay, mister, where did it come from this time?"

"The Internet," said Cory with a shrug. "If the Boyz touched it, you can sell it. Napkins, straws, maybe even a lock of hair."

Mrs. Baxter exchanged a shocked look with her husband. "Cory," she said sternly, "why didn't you tell us about this?"

Cory studied his parents' unhappy faces. "I'm sorry. Are you guys mad?"

"Yeah," said Mrs. Baxter, "mad we didn't think of it first!"

"Hey, honey," said Mr. Baxter, "did you wash their towels?"

Mrs. Baxter's face brightened. "Not yet."

Mr. Baxter took off for the laundry room.

"And don't forget the pillowcases!" Mrs. Baxter yelled after him. "Hey, you didn't take out the garbage yet, did you?"

"Oh, snap!" her husband cried.